RATCHET & CLANK™

WITHDRAWN

Hero Time

Adapted by Meredith Rusu
From the script by T.J. Fixman, Gerry Swallow, and Kevin Munroe
Based on characters created by Insomniac Games

© 2016 Sony Computer Entertainment America LLC. Ratchet & Clank characters © Sony Computer Entertainment America LLC. Ratchet & Clank movie © 2015 Ratchet Productions, LLC.

Published by Scholastic Inc., *Publishers since 1920.* SCHOLASTIC and associated logos are trademarks and/or registered trademarks of Scholastic Inc.

ISBN 978-1-338-03042-6

12 11 10 9 8 7 6 5 4 3 2 1   16 17 18 19 20

Printed in the U.S.A.   40
First printing 2016

SCHOLASTIC INC.

Far out in the Solana Galaxy, an alien named Chairman Drek had a plan. And it was not a nice one.

"Activate the Deplanetizer!" he told his troops.

In a flash, his spacecraft fired a superpowered laser beam at an empty planet.

KA-BOOM!

The planet exploded!

"Heh, heh, heh." Drek just needed to destroy a few more planets, and he would have all the pieces he needed to complete his master plan. No one in the galaxy could stop him now.

Meanwhile, on the planet Veldin, a Lombax named Ratchet did push-ups. "And one . . . and two . . . I'm on fire!" Ratchet exclaimed.

Suddenly, a news broadcast interrupted his workout program. "This just in," said the announcer. "Planet Tenemule is no more!"

"What?" Ratchet cried. This was the fourth empty planet destroyed in a week.

"To help with the investigation, the Galactic Rangers are looking for a new recruit," the announcer continued.

Ratchet gasped. "Ranger tryouts!"

All his life, Ratchet had been a mechanic. And a pretty good one, too. But deep down, he dreamed of becoming a Galactic Ranger.

Ratchet begged his boss, Grimroth, for time off to go to the tryouts.

"Please, Grim. I just feel like I'm supposed to do something more."

Reluctantly, Grim said yes.

Soon, Ratchet was at the tryouts. He couldn't believe how many people were there!

"Ladies and gentlemen!" a loud voice announced. "Give a big Planet Veldin welcome to your . . . GALACTIC RANGERS!"

The announcer introduced the Galactic Rangers one by one.

"She'll shoot first and ask questions when she's good and ready . . . Cora Veralux!

"You loved him at Grapplemania. You love him more as a Galactic Ranger. Get ready for Brax Lectrus!

"And finally, ladies and gentlemen, the savior of Solana, Captain Qwark!"

Ratchet was totally stoked. He just *knew* he had what it took to become a Galactic Ranger!

"You don't have what it takes." Captain Qwark told Ratchet in the tryout room.

"Please, just give me a chance," Ratchet said.

Qwark shook his head. "You're inexperienced, and you've broken a lot of rules."

"Possession of an illegal gravity repulsor," Cora read from Ratchet's profile. "Willful disruption of the space-time continuum?"

Ratchet laughed nervously. "*That* is a funny story."

"You're a loose canon," said Qwark. "And that's *my* shtick."

Ratchet slumped in his seat. His big chance was over before it had even begun.

Meanwhile, across the galaxy, Chairman Drek was planning his next move. The Galactic Rangers were guarding the next planet he wanted to destroy. So he asked an evil mastermind named Dr. Nefarious to help him.

Nefarious *used* to be a Galactic Ranger. But Qwark had teased him for being a nerd. Now Nefarious wanted revenge.

Doctor Nefarious presented Drek with a robot army.

"Three hundred warbots," he exclaimed. "Built using the rarest metal in the galaxy, and programmed to destroy the Galactic Rangers!"

Nefarious didn't know it, but one of his robots was defective. A power surge had occurred while he was being assembled. He was tiny, and although he had been programmed to defeat the Rangers, he wanted to help them.

The little robot's name was Clank. He escaped from Drek's factory and leaped into a space pod.

"Computer, set coordinates for the Galactic Ranger home base," he instructed.

But the ship was damaged. It went in the wrong direction.

"Oh, dear," said Clank.

Clank crashed onto Planet Veldin. Luckily, Ratchet saw his ship fall out of the sky. He pulled the little robot to safety just as the space pod exploded.

"Easy there," Ratchet told him. "You've been in a crash. Let me fix you up."

He brought Clank to his workshop and repaired the robot's circuits.

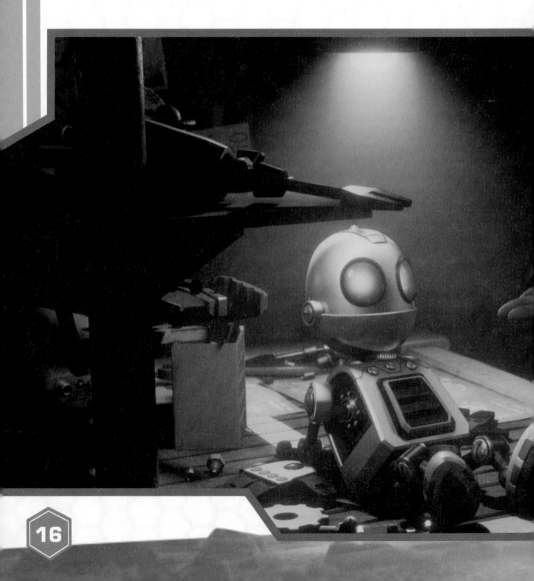

"Thank you," said Clank. "Now I must get to Aleero City. Chairman Drek has built an army of warbots. They are going to destroy the Galactic Rangers tomorrow."

"No way!" said Ratchet. "We have to warn them before it's too late!"

Ratchet and Clank flew to Aleero City. But when they got there, the Rangers were already under attack.

"There are too many of them," said Brax as the warbots surrounded them.

"Hold steady, Rangers," commanded Qwark.

Things weren't looking good.

"Ratchet, I have an idea," said Clank. "Your ship has a Mag-Booster."

"Good thinking, Clank!" cried Ratchet. They could use the Mag-Booster as a magnet to attract the warbots' metal. Then Ratchet and Clank could fling the warbots into space!

With just a few adjustments, they engaged the Mag-Booster, and . . .

CLANG! CLANG! CLANG!

One by one, the warbots flew up to the ship and away from the Galactic Rangers.

Down in Aleero City, everyone cheered. They wanted to meet the heroes who had saved the day.

But Captain Qwark wasn't happy. He didn't like two hotshots stealing his moment in the spotlight.

"Captain Qwark," called a news reporter. "Will these heroes be joining the Rangers?"

Qwark gasped. He *really* didn't like that! But everyone was watching. "I . . . I don't see why not!"

Ratchet was thrilled. His dream of becoming a Ranger was coming true!

Over the next few days, Ratchet began Ranger training. He got a new protosuit. He practiced using fancy weapons. He even got a jet pack.

"Wicked!" said Ratchet.

Meanwhile, the Rangers' science officer, Elaris, had figured out Drek was behind the exploding planets.

"Okay, Rangers," said Qwark. "Our plan is simple. We'll HALO drop into Drek Industries, fire a whole bunch of weapons, and take Drek into custody."

Clank and Elaris thought the plan sounded too easy to work. But Qwark wouldn't listen. So off the Rangers went.

The plan *was* too easy to work. In fact, it was a mess!

Enemy robots quickly separated the Rangers. Drek cornered Qwark in his office. He had a sneaky trick up his sleeve.

"I think it's dreadful what Ratchet has done to you," Drek told Qwark. "He's made people forget who the real hero is. It's time you joined us."

"I could never betray the people of Solana," Qwark said.

"Betraying them is how you get them to LOVE you!" said Drek.

Drek explained that everyone would think Qwark was a victim. An innocent superhero pushed to go bad . . . all because of Ratchet.

"No one needs to get hurt," said Drek. "Do we have a deal?"

Meanwhile, the other Rangers had found Drek's main computer lab.

"Fascinating," Clank said. "These plans show that Drek is collecting pieces to *build* the perfect planet."

The next target was the planet Novalis.

Cora's face went pale. "Millions of people live on Novalis!"

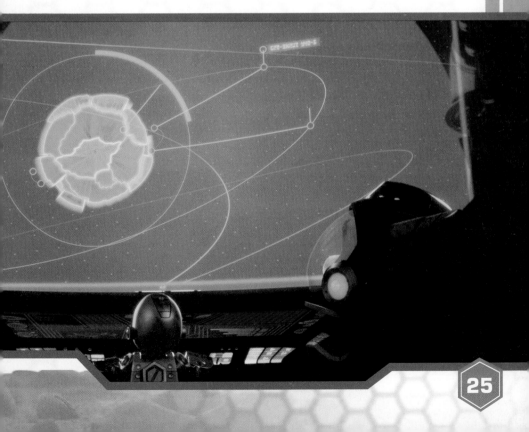

Qwark and the Rangers zoomed off. They had
to defend Novalis while the people there fled.

"What's the plan, Captain?" Cora asked.

"Oh, uh, I'll go in first and reason with Drek,"
said Qwark.

Qwark flew down to the Deplanetizer. Cora,
Brax, Elaris, Ratchet, and Clank had no idea he
was working against them. Even worse, Qwark had
sabotaged the Rangers' weapons!

"You performed marvelously," Drek told Qwark.

"I have your word my team won't get hurt?" Qwark asked nervously.

Drek grinned. "Captain, where's the trust?"

The moment Qwark was onboard the Deplanetizer, Drek commanded his troops. "Destroy the Rangers!"

His troops opened fire!

"We've been sabotaged!" cried Elaris. "Fall back!"

"But we can't leave Qwark!" Ratchet said.

Ratchet zoomed down to the Deplanetizer. He had to stop the laser beam and save Qwark. He had to be a hero!

KA-BOOM!

Drek trapped him in a containment sphere!

"Bravo, my boy!" Drek sneered. "The next time you Rangers decide to play hero, plan better."

"Drek, don't do this," Ratchet pleaded. "Novalis is home to millions."

Just then, Ratchet spotted Qwark. Unlike Ratchet, he wasn't a prisoner. He was safe and sound!

"Qwark?" Ratchet asked in disbelief.

Drek cackled. "Captain Qwark is on our side now." He turned to a trooper. "Toss Ratchet into one of those shuttles. I want him to live to see his failure."

"No!" Ratchet cried. But it was no use. He watched helplessly as the Deplanetizer fired. Novalis was destroyed!

Ratchet hung his head. Everyone had left Novalis, but the people had lost their home. He had failed. Some hero he had turned out to be.

Back onboard the Deplanetizer, Qwark was angry at Drek.

"You tried to kill my Rangers," he said. "You said you'd leave them alone."

Just then, Dr. Nefarious walked in.

"You're working with Nefarious?" Qwark gasped. "You have no idea how evil he is."

"Oh, but I do," Drek said.

"What was your price for selling out your friends?" Nefarious asked Qwark.

Qwark felt ashamed. Nefarious was right. He was a bad guy now.

Back on Veldin, Ratchet had returned to Grim's workshop. He was miserable.

The Rangers were all trying to contact him. They wanted him to return. But Ratchet didn't have the heart to face them.

Grim tried to make him feel better.

"I guess I just wanted to do something big," Ratchet told him. "I wanted to matter."

"I've never been very good with advice," said Grim. "But I do know this. To be a hero, you don't need to do big things. Just the right ones."

Just then, Clank and the Galactic Rangers arrived. They had come to take Ratchet back.

"I'm sorry I ran out on you," Ratchet said.

"We've all made bad choices," Cora said.

"Drek has one more target," said Clank. "With Qwark working for the enemy, we need you more than ever."

"But how are we going to stop him?" asked Ratchet.

"Well, we can't move a planet out of the way," said Elaris. "But what if we could move the weapon targeting that planet?"

Ratchet looked up at the Mag-Booster on his old ship.

"Guys, I have an idea."

Ratchet and Clank worked together to fix the Mag-Booster.

In the meantime, Elaris had figured out Drek's final target. It was a planet called Umbris. No one lived there, but the planet was unstable. If it exploded, it would destroy the entire galaxy.

Then the Rangers discovered that Umbris wasn't
Drek's idea. It was Dr. Nefarious's! He wanted
revenge on the Rangers, so he was using Drek to
destroy the galaxy!

Ratchet and Clank disguised themselves
as Qwark. Together, they sneaked onboard the
Deplanetizer and disconnected the weapon's
stabilizer. Without it, Cora and Brax could use the
Mag-Booster to knock the Deplanetizer off course.

But just as they were escaping . . .

"Greetings, cadet!" Captain Qwark appeared behind Ratchet and Clank.

Ratchet couldn't hold back his anger. "You stabbed your own team in the back, Qwark!"

"Just like you stabbed me in the back," Qwark shot back. "Taking my fans, my sponsors . . . my parking space!!"

"You were my hero!" Ratchet exclaimed. "Now you're no better than Nefarious."

Qwark gasped. "How *dare* you. I am way better-looking than Nefarious!"

Ratchet was done arguing. "Captain Qwark, on behalf of the Galactic Rangers, I'm placing you under arrest."

Ratchet used all his Ranger skills to battle Qwark. But the captain used Dr. Nefarious's powerful Tornado Launcher to trap him.

"Qwark, please, stop!" Ratchet begged. "Nefarious is tricking you. He wants to destroy the galaxy. If Umbris explodes everyone will die, including us. Is that how you want to be remembered?"

Qwark realized Ratchet was right. He shut down the Tornado Launcher.

"I'm sorry," he said. "I don't know how everything got this far."

"This is just pathetic!" came a voice from above them.

· It was Dr. Nefarious!

"Give it up," said Qwark. "We're placing you under arrest."

"Think again," said Nefarious. "You're not a hero! You're not even a good villain. You're the galaxy's biggest joke. And now, everyone will know!"

Before Ratchet and Qwark could stop him, Nefarious activated the Deplanetizer!

Up above, Cora and Brax had engaged the Mag-Booster. Together, they pulled the Deplanetizer off course.

"It's working!" cried Cora.

The Deplanetizer fired—and missed Umbris! Instead, it hit the new planet Drek had created, vaporizing it.

Drek's plan was foiled, and the galaxy was saved.

"No! My plan!" screamed Nefarious. "You ruined my plan!"

Furious, the doctor pointed his deadliest weapon at the captain. "You've had this one coming a long time, Qwark."

But Ratchet ran up behind him. "Hey, Nefarious!"
With one powerful swing, Ratchet knocked
Nefarious off the platform.

"Noooooo!" screamed Nefarious as he fell into
the Deplanetizer's core. He vanished in a bright
flash of light.

Back onboard the Rangers' ship, everyone celebrated.

Qwark knew he had a galactic apology tour ahead of him. "How many planets do you think I'll have to save before they call me a hero again?"

"You don't have to do big things to be a hero," Ratchet told him. "Just the right ones."

As for Ratchet, he had had enough of being a hero. For now.

"But if there's ever trouble again, I'll be ready," he declared. "Once a Ranger, always a Ranger!"